THE

Snow Globe

MURDER

THE
Snow Globe
MURDER

PENELOPE LOVELETTER

LOVELETTER
PUBLICATIONS
EST. 2023

Original Text by Penelope Loveletter
The moral rights of the author have been asserted.
Cover design by Penelope Loveletter

Copyright 2024, Penelope Loveletter

All rights reserved. No part of this publication may be reproduced, stored in a retrieval system, or transmitted, in any form or by any means, electronic, mechanical, photocopying, recording or otherwise, without the prior written permission of the publisher and copyright owner.

Other Books by
Penelope Loveletter

<u>Whispering Pines Sweet Romances:</u>
Whispers by the Lake
Whispers of the Heart
Whispers of Forever

<u>Whispering Pines Cozy Mysteries:</u>
Whispers of Murder
Whispers of Death
Whispers of Mystery
Whispers in the Dark

<u>Whispers in Europe Cozy Mysteries:</u>
Macarons and Murder
Meringues and Murder

Dedicated to Alan
Forever

♡

Chapter 1

Rose Bennett's hands trembled as she positioned a vintage magnifying glass against a stack of gleaming new cozy mystery novels in the front window of The Literary Cat. Through the glass, snow drifted onto Main Street, coating the empty sidewalks of Whispering Pines in pristine white. It was not yet seven in the morning, but Rose had been in her new shop for over an hour putting finishing touches on book arrangements, adjusting the displays in the front windows, and making sure there wasn't a speck of dust on any of the shelves. Everything had to be perfect for the grand opening.

Christie, her cream-colored ragdoll cat purred as she twined herself around Rose's ankles and leapt gracefully into the window display.

"Christie, no!" Rose lunged to catch a length of silver garland as Christie batted it off a wooden display stand beside a display of classics. "Oh, my gosh. That's the third time this morning!"

Christie blinked up at her with innocent blue eyes before draping herself on the window ledge, tail swishing across the carefully arranged book covers.

Rose sighed and tucked an escaped curl behind her ear as she turned to her other cat.

"What do you think, Agatha?" She glanced at her lilac-point ragdoll, sprawled across an overstuffed armchair. "Too cluttered?"

Agatha responded by rolling onto her back and stretching a paw tinted with the lightest grey toward the garland hanging from the mantle. Rose grinned and turned just in time to see Christie reaching one paw under the magnifying glass on the cozy mystery display, sliding it precariously close to the edge.

"Oh no you don't." Rose rescued the antique prop and readjusted the stack of books. As she moved a display poster for a book signing next week she said, "I know you two think this is elaborate cat toy storage, but-"

A sharp sting shot through her finger as the edge of the poster sliced her skin.

"Oh!" she gasped at the sight of bright red welling up from the paper cut. Rose grabbed the counter for support, her knees threatening to buckle. "Oh no. This is ridiculous," she said, fumbling for the first aid kit under the register. "I read murder mysteries for fun but can't handle the sight of a paper cut."

She wrapped the bandage around her finger with shaking hands while both cats watched with tilted heads.

"Don't judge me," Rose told them, steadying herself against the counter. "Everyone's allowed one irrational fear. Even if it doesn't make sense for someone who owns every Agatha Christie novel ever written."

Christie responded by coming to brush against Rose's legs with a purr.

"You two are amazing," Rose said as she bent to pet Christie's white and cream fur.

A crash from the fireplace made Rose jump. Agatha had not only pulled down the silver garland but managed to tangle it around her ears.

"Amazing troublemakers," Rose said with a laugh as she finished securing the band-aid around her finger. Christie followed as Rose untangled Agatha and began replacing the garland. "Apparently dangling this from the mantle is too much of a temptation," she said as she took the garland from Agatha's playful paws.

As Rose turned toward the window, she saw the corner of something brown on the front doorstep. She set the garland aside and walked to window to look out. Through the glass, she could see a brown box beside her door, partially covered in snow.

Rose pulled out her keys and opened the heavy oak door. A blast of winter air swept inside as she snatched up the package. Her fingers tingled from the cold dampness that had seeped into the brown paper.

Back inside, she set the mystery box on the counter next to her register. Water droplets from the melting snow fell onto the wood counter. She turned the package, searching for a return address or shipping label, but found nothing except her own name written in an elegant script.

A cream-colored envelope was taped to the top. Rose's heart quickened. She hadn't expected any grand opening gifts. She'd only been in Whispering Pines for three weeks, barely long enough to learn the names of the other shop owners on Main Street.

She slipped her finger under the envelope's flap, careful to avoid another paper cut. The card inside was simple white card stock with just four words written in the same flowing script: "Happy grand opening, Rose!"

"How mysterious!" She flipped the card over, but the back was blank. "What do you think, Agatha? Should we open it?"

From her new perch atop the fireplace mantel, Agatha blinked slowly, the garland now draped across her back like a silver shawl.

Rose nodded. "I agree." She sliced through the brown paper with her letter opener, revealing a pristine white box tied with a silver ribbon. Her fingers traced the silky bow before untying it.

She lifted the lid and pulled back layers of silver tissue paper. Nestled inside sat a snow globe. As she lifted it from its cushioned bed, it caught the early morning light streaming through her window. Her breath caught.

The base was carved wood with delicate silver snowflakes painted around the edge. But it was the scene inside that made her gasp. There, in perfect miniature detail, stood The Literary Cat - a tiny red house with white trim and shutters, complete with the curved pathway leading to the front door. Even the snow-covered bushes were recreated in exquisite detail.

"Agatha, Christie - come look at this!" Rose turned the globe slowly, marveling at how the artist had captured every architectural detail, right down to the decorative molding above the windows. When she shook it gently, glittering snow swirled around the little bookstore.

Christie padded over and batted curiously at the tissue paper that had fallen to the floor, while Rose set the snow globe on the counter. Who could have sent such a thoughtful gift? She'd only met a handful of people since moving to Whispering Pines. Mrs. Chen from the tea shop next door had been welcoming, but they'd barely exchanged more than pleasant greetings. And Abigail, who owned the soap and candle shop on the south side of The Literary Cat, was a single mom with a toddler and a business to run. Surely she didn't have time or money for a gift like this. The elderly couple who owned the hardware store had helped her hang shelves, but this didn't seem their style. As she looked back at the card, she wondered, why no signature?

Rose picked up the globe again. The craftsmanship was incredible - this wasn't some mass-produced souvenir. Someone had carefully crafted this piece specifically for her store.

She gently placed it in her front window display next to the collection of vintage Agatha Christie novels. It caught the morning light perfectly adding just the right touch of wonder to her grand opening decorations.

"I wonder who could have sent it?"

Chapter 2

A sharp knock at the door made Rose jump. Christie darted under the nearest reading chair while Agatha merely stretched on her mantle perch, unbothered.

Through the glass, Rose spotted Bridget from Northern Pines Bakery, her dark hair dusted with snowflakes balancing two paper cups and a white bakery bag in her hands.

Rose opened the door and flipped the sign on the door from 'Closed' to 'Open.' "You're out early!"

"Had to catch you before the crowds." Bridget swept in, bringing the scent of cinnamon and fresh coffee with her. Her cheeks were pink from the cold. "Thought you might need some fuel for your big day."

"You're amazing." Rose accepted the steaming cup and breathed in the rich aroma. "I was so nervous about setting up, I completely forgot breakfast."

Bridget set the bakery bag on the counter. "Fresh cinnamon roll - still warm." She pulled a stack of pale pink cards from her apron pocket. "And I brought these. Ten percent off at the bakery. Thought your customers might like them?"

"Of course! That's so thoughtful." Rose cleared a spot near the register for the coupons. "Though if they try your cinnamon rolls, they probably won't need much convincing to visit."

Christie emerged from her hiding spot, nose twitching at the sweet smell. Bridget laughed and scratched behind the cat's ears. "I see someone else wants breakfast too."

"These two are spoiled enough." Rose took a sip of coffee, letting the warmth spread through her. "But thank you, really. This is exactly what I needed this morning."

"Don't even think about it." Bridget adjusted the garland on the mantle and reached for Agatha, who immediately melted into her arms with a rumbling purr.

"Besides, what's the point of having a friend open a bookstore if you can't spoil her a little?"

Rose's throat tightened. After months of wondering if she'd made the right choice leaving her corporate job in Minneapolis, Bridget's words hit home. She hadn't just bought a bookstore - she'd found budding friendships in this small town.

"Your window's coming along beautifully," Bridget said, scratching under Agatha's chin. "Though I see that these two have been 'helping.'" She nodded to Christie and Agatha.

"Christie knocked over my stack of vintage Agatha Christie novels twice already. And now this one-" Rose gestured at Agatha, who had closed her eyes in contentment, "decided the garland made a better toy than decoration."

"At least they're living up to their namesakes - leaving a trail of mysteries to solve." Bridget laughed as Agatha stretched one paw to bat Bridget's long brown braid. "The store looks amazing," she said, taking in the cozy reading nooks and carefully arranged shelves.

"I hope everyone else thinks so too." Rose twisted her hands together. "I'm terrified no one will come. But can I ask you a question? You didn't, by any chance, leave a package on my doorstep, did you?"

Bridget looked confused, so Rose hurried on. "I mean, I found a box outside this morning. And I don't know who it's from. Look at this."

She showed Bridget the snow globe, and Bridget's eyes grew wide. "This is amazing! That's your shop!"

"I know. It's incredible. But there was no name on the card. I don't know who left it."

Before Bridget could respond, the door chimed, and Wilma Olson and Sarah Winters entered. Sarah clutched a Northern Pines Bakery coffee cup wrapped in a napkin secured by a rubber band. Mrs. Olson took off her mittens and dropped them into her book bag. They were, Rose knew, next door neighbors. She felt herself let out a breath. Actual customers were arriving!

"I declare, this is exactly what Whispering Pines needs," Wilma exclaimed. "No more driving to Silver Pines when I need a new book!"

"And you have a fireplace!" Sarah said. "This looks like the perfect place to unwind after the stress of my dissertation."

Sarah motioned to her coffee cup. "Are we allowed to bring these in?"

Rose smiled. "Of course. This is a place to be comfy and enjoy books."

Sarah wandered around the main room of the store, admiring the books, the fireplace, and the window display.

"And you're a cat person?" Wilma asked.

Rose smiled. "I am! Do you have cats?"

Wilma nodded "A black cat named Midnight. She was a gift from my granddaughters, Gwendolyn and Ali."

"Where's your fiction section?" Sarah asked. "I could use something to take my mind off school."

"Right by the fireplace," Rose said as she lifted Christie from the window and carried her back to the kitchen where she deposited her with a gentle nudge, hoping she might settle in her favorite cushion on the antique chair.

The kitchen door barely had time to close before the front door jingled again and a young woman and an older man stepped inside. She shook snow from her long, dark ponytail and his tweed jacket was dusted with snow.

"Welcome to town," the young woman said warmly. "I heard we had a bookstore opening today and had to come check it out on my way to work!"

Bridget rushed forward and hugged the young woman. "This is Isabella Chang, Rose. She works at the bank. She has the best sense of humor in town."

Isabella laughed and shook her head. "I don't know about that. But I am always up for having fun."

"I've been thinking of hosting a game night here once a month," Rose said. "Would you be interested?"

"I'd love to come to a game night," Isabella said. "I'll just have a peek around this morning before I head over to the bank."

The older man grunted and looked around with a scowl. "Kind of small, isn't it?"

Startled, Rose said, "Well, it is cozy. But we have more rooms in the back. There's a children's section, the non-fiction room with science, travel, and history, and one room just for cookbooks and crafting."

With an almost imperceptible eye roll, Bridget said, "This is Professor Ed Mitchell. Ed, meet Rose Bennett, our newest business owner."

The professor gave a small grunt and extended his hand. "Well, at least you have a history section."

"Professor Mitchell teaches history at the university," Bridget said. "Medieval Europe is his specialty."

"Medieval Europe?" Rose said. "Fascinating. I have a small collection of history books. Would you like to see our non-fiction room?" She gestured toward the doorway. "It's not a university library, of course, but I did try to get a few interesting titles."

Professor Mitchell nodded as the front door opened again, letting in a gust of cold air and more customers.

Rose guided the professor through the main room. She smiled when she saw that Sarah was settling into one of the armchairs with a novel. This was what she had hoped for- people setting in with books, finding the sections of the store they loved, and hopefully feeling so at home that they would return for the atmosphere as much as the books.

In the non-fiction room, sunlight streamed through the window, illuminating the beautifully arranged shelves.

"The history section is on these three bookcases," Rose explained, pointing to the shelves along the far wall. "I've organized them by era and region. Medieval Europe is right here." She ran her finger along the spines of several thick volumes.

Professor Mitchell adjusted his glasses and leaned in to examine the titles. "Well. This is actually impressive for a small bookstore. You have Duby's work on medieval agriculture - that's not something you find just anywhere."

Rose smiled. "I'm so glad you know it!" Through the doorway, she heard the bell jingle again. "Have a look around and let me know if there's anything in particular you'd like me to order in for you!"

Throughout the morning, more townspeople came in. Some Rose knew, some she had seen in passing, and some she had never met but hoped would become regular customers and friends.

"Rose is going to know everyone in Whispering Pines before the day is through," Bridget said with a laugh as her the owner of the bakery, Emma, paused to admire the window display. "She even got Ed Mitchell to smile."

Emma raised an eyebrow. "So you work miracles, do you?" she said with a wink. In a whisper, she added, "That man has managed to collect more enemies in town than Betty Wilson has plants in her garden."

The door chimed again, and Rose looked over. The man in the doorway had snowflakes dusting his thick brown hair and although it was not yet noon, he had a hint of a 5 o'clock shadow. His handsome features broke into a warm smile as he caught her staring.

"Uh, hi. Welcome to The Literary Cat," Rose said, her voice coming out higher than intended.

"Jack Hilton." He held out his hand and Rose dropped a book to take it.

"Rose," she said. "Welcome to my bookstore." She cringed as she bent to pick up the dropped book. That sounded ridiculous.

But Jack didn't seem to notice. He crouched down as Agatha trotted over to investigate him, her tail held high. "Wow. Beautiful cat. Is she a ragdoll?"

Rose felt herself relax a bit. Handsome men always seemed to make her nervous, but she could talk about her cats with anyone. "That's Agatha. Christie's around here somewhere too." Rose tucked a curl behind her ear, watching his strong hands gently pet Agatha's fur.

"Both ragdolls?" Jack set his coffee cup on the floor beside him as Agatha flopped onto her side, exposing her belly.

"Yes, sisters. Christie's a cream point, but she's probably hiding in the kitchen. She's more shy with new people."

"Unlike this sweetheart." Jack scratched under Agatha's chin. "I see plenty of cats, but ragdolls are special. Such personalities-"

Rose nodded. "They're my babies! You know cat breeds well, it looks like."

He smiled up at her. "I'm a vet. And I have a soft spot for cats."

"Here? In Whispering Pines?"

He nodded and Rose let out a happy laugh. "And I was worried I might have to drive back into the Twin Cities for vet care. This is great news! I mean, if you're accepting new clients." She felt her cheeks flush. "Are you accepting new clients?"

He shook his head. "I'm not right now. My receptionist and assistant, Jill, made me promise not to take any more clients until we can get another vet tech. There are a lot of pets in Whispering Pines, and until I can find an assistant, it's just me and Jill."

Jill. Rose felt her heart wilt a bit. He was apparently taken. Not surprisingly.

As Jack turned to follow Agatha, his elbow knocked the coffee cup spilling dark liquid across the hardwood floor.

"Oh no, I'm so sorry!" Jack jumped up, nearly tripping over Agatha.

"It's fine, I'll grab paper towels-"

"Please, let me clean it up." Jack held up his hands. "I deal with much worse messes at the clinic. Though usually they're not my fault." His eyes crinkled at the corners as he smiled sheepishly. "Hazard of being chronically clumsy with coffee cups, I'm afraid."

Rose felt her cheeks warm at his smile. "Paper towels are in the kitchen. Through that door."

"Thanks. And when I find an assistant, I'd love to care for your cats. Promise I'm not always this clumsy." He winked as he headed for the kitchen.

"At least it wasn't near any books!" Rose called after him, her heart still fluttering as her shop-neighbor, Abigail, tried to keep her toddler, Jamison, from chasing the cat through the spilled coffee.

Betty Wilson, an older woman, was examining the plant guides with a critical eye. "Do you have anything on Asian peonies?" she asked Rose, who admitted she didn't as she moved Agatha out of the way so Jack could wipe up the coffee.

Chelsea Evans, the mechanic who had changed Rose's oil last week, came in and gave Rose a quick hug. "So today's the big day!" She was wearing jeans and a sweater instead of her coveralls. "Do you have a history section, by any chance?" Rose pointed her to the non-fiction room as Christie, tail held high, emerged from the kitchen and wove between Betty Wilson's ankles.

"Get back," Betty said sternly. "Have you no animal instincts? I am not a cat person!"

"Sorry about that," Rose said as she scooped Christie into her arms. Her nerves were a bit frayed. This was a lot to handle and already, and Rose was wondering if *she* needed to hire an assistant. A busy grand opening was wonderful, but if every day was like this, she would need help.

Betty sniffed. "I have the sweetest little dog. Beverly. I don't suppose you allow dogs in the store?" When Rose hesitated, glancing at the cat in her arms, Betty said, "I could never stand cats. They have no sense of personal space."

Rose gave a tight smile. "I'd love to meet your dog some time."

"Beverly is a special dog," Jack said as he carried a handful of soaked paper towels into the kitchen.

Betty gave Jack a smile in response before she gathered her stack of gardening books and pushed past Rose into the non-fiction room.

"Do you have any children's books?" Abigail asked, still trying to stop Jamison from chasing the cats.

"I do! Come with me." Rose led Abigail and her young son to the side room where children's books and stuffed animals stood among a collection of comfy second-hand furniture and beanbags.

"Jamison, look! It's *The Little Blue Truck*!"

As Rose turned, Betty huffed out of the non-fiction room, gardening books still in her arms. "Insufferable know-it-all," she muttered under her breath. "You didn't tell me Ed was back there."

Rose raised her eyebrows, but Bridget gave her a small smile and shook her head.

"It's just Betty," she whispered. "I don't think she can stand anyone. I mean, except her horrible little pug dog."

Rose laughed as the bell over the door jingled again and a young couple she didn't recognize came in, shaking snow from their hair, cheeks pink from the cold. It was turning out to be a better grand opening than Rose had even dared imagine.

Chapter 3

That evening, the winter sun hung low in the sky, casting long shadows through the front windows. Rose's feet ached from a successful first day, but her heart was light. She waved goodbye to Chelsea, who'd emerged from the non-fiction room with two books on Norse mythology that she'd bought.

"Last call for books," Rose announced to the remaining browsers. "We're closing in fifteen minutes."

As the final customers drifted out into the snowy evening, books in hand, the streetlight out front flickered on. Agatha settled herself back in the chair by the fire, wrapped her tail around her nose, and gazed up at the garland. Rose looked around for Christie and found her lying on the floor by the non-fiction room door, her cream-colored tail twitching.

Christie let out a plaintive *meow*.

"What's wrong, sweet girl?" Rose asked, gathering empty coffee cups from various surfaces and tossing them into the trash can.

Christie meowed again, and Rose smiled. "Dinner will have to wait until I get things tidied up. I think you'll survive."

But as she straightened the poster in the front window, Rose stopped. Her new snow globe wasn't where she had set it. She scanned the display, but it wasn't there. Someone must have moved it.

Rose frowned. She looked at the cash register counter, and then at the mantle. It wasn't there, either. Why would anyone have moved her snow globe?

Christie more insistently as Rose scanned the room for the snow globe. It wasn't on the end tables, or, as far as she could see, perched on any of the bookshelves. That was good. It might brake if it fell.

Christie scratched at the bottom of the non-fiction room door and Agatha jumped lightly off the chair and joined her, reaching one paw under the door and meowing.

Rose suddenly realized the door was closed.

"That's also odd," she said as she hurried over and scooped both cats into her arms. "Are you starving? You silly girls. And who closed this door, hmm?"

Rose deposited the cats in the kitchen before returning to the door. She tried to turn the handle, but it was locked.

"What on earth?" She pulled her keys in her cardigan pocket, certain she hadn't used them since opening up that morning.

Christie trotted out of the kitchen and let out another urgent meow.

"Okay, okay." Rose fumbled with her key ring, trying to find the right key. she inserted it. "Give me a minute. Dinner is coming." The lock clicked open, and the door swung inward.

Rose's breath caught in her throat.

Professor Mitchell lay sprawled on his back beside the history shelves, spots of red on the carpet beside him. Next to his outstretched hand, her new snow globe lay shattered, its liquid seeping into the carpet. The tiny red and white house had broken free from its base.

Rose's knees went weak at the sight of blood matting his silver-streaked hair. The room tilted. She gripped the doorframe to steady herself, her other hand pressed against her mouth, as she looked away.

Christie darted between her feet and sniffed at the professor's tweed jacket.

"Professor Mitchell?" Rose's voice came out as a whisper. When he didn't respond, she forced herself to look at him again, fighting the wave of nausea that threatened to overwhelm her.

"Oh heavens," she whispered. "He can't be.... dead."

Chapter 4

Rose stumbled backward, her fingers white-knuckled on the doorframe. Dark spots danced at the edges of her vision as she glanced quickly at the drops of crimson soaking into the cream-colored carpet. Her stomach lurched.

Don't faint. Don't faint. Don't faint.

She spun away from the doorway, legs wobbling as she hurried back through the main room. The flames in the fireplace blurred and doubled in her vision. She collapsed into the wingback chair, her heart hammering against her ribs.

Her phone slipped in her clammy fingers, and she missed the emergency dial buttons twice before managing to hit the numbers.

"911, what's your emergency?"

Rose's voice came out thin and shaky. "I need help. There's a man... he's not moving. There's blood." She pressed her free hand to her forehead, willing the room to stop spinning.

When the woman asked her location, it took Rose a moment to remember. "The Literary Cat Bookstore on Main Street in Whispering Pines."

Agatha padded over and batted at a crumpled napkin near Rose's feet, her lilac-tipped tail curling around Rose's ankle. Christie leapt onto Rose's lap, pressing her warm weight against Rose's stomach. Rose buried her trembling fingers in Christie's thick fur.

"Ma'am, is the person breathing?"

Rose's throat tightened. "I... I don't know. I couldn't... there was blood. I can't handle blood. I almost passed out."

"Stay on the line. Officers and paramedics are on their way. Are you alone in the building?"

"Yes. Well, no. My cats are here." Rose stroked Christie's head, focusing on the soft fur beneath her fingers rather than the image of Professor Mitchell lying motionless on her bookstore floor. "Just... please hurry."

Red and blue lights flashed through the front windows, painting dancing shadows across the bookshelves. Rose hugged Christie closer as heavy boots clomped up the front steps. Before they could knock, Rose hurried over to open the door.

A blonde female officer in a navy uniform stepped inside, her hand hovering near her weapon. "Are you Rose Bennett?"

"Yes." Rose's voice cracked.

The officer's blue eyes swept over Rose and then around the room. "I'm Officer Lindberg. Are you hurt?"

Rose shook her head. "No, I just... I found him."

"Him?"

"Professor Mitchell. He's on the floor. There's blood. He's not conscious." Rose tried to stop her voice from trembling and her knees from shaking as she led the way to the non-fiction room.

More officers and paramedics flooded in, their equipment clattering against doorframes. They rushed past Rose while Officer Lindberg, after glancing into the non-fiction room at the professor, led Rose back to the chairs beside the fireplace. Agatha jumped up and settled on the woman's lap, and Officer Lindberg gave her a quick pet before she pulled out a notepad.

"Can you tell me what happened?"

Rose described the door being locked, Christie meowing, and her finding Professor Mitchell. "My new snow globe is-" she shook her head trying not to think about the blood, "-is broken. I think it was used to hit him. He's not, he can't be...?"

"We'll let the paramedics handle that," Officer Lindberg said gently as a camera flash lit up the non-fiction room's doorway.

"Can you tell me who else was in the store today?" Officer Lindberg asked.

"Well, yes. Customers! I think half the town was here. It was my grand opening." Rose twisted Christie's fur between her fingers. "Oh gosh. It went really well. Or I thought it had. I had so many people here. But now this..." Her voice trailed off and she started shaking.

Before Officer Lindberg could answer, the paramedics emerged wheeling a stretcher. A white sheet covered the still form beneath. Rose's chest tightened.

"Does that mean...?"

"I'm sorry." Officer Lindberg's voice softened. "It looks like he didn't make it."

Rose pressed her face into Christie's fur as tears welled up. The officers continued taking photos and notes, moving from the non-fiction room into the main room.

"We'll need to ask more questions," Officer Lindberg said. "But I think it can wait until morning. You've been through enough tonight." She glanced around the store. "Do you live nearby? Would you like someone to take you home, to stay with you?"

"I live upstairs." Rose gestured toward the back of the store. "My kitchen's behind the shop but my bedroom and living room are upstairs. I'll be fine with my cats. But thank you."

Officer Lindberg tipped her head. "Are you sure? I can get someone to stay with you. This is a lot to take in."

Rose shook her head, and Office Lindberg nodded. "Here's my card. Call me if you need anything. Even if you just want someone to stay here in the store with you."

Rose swallowed the lump in her throat. "Thank you. I just want to get upstairs. I'll be alright."

After everyone had left, Rose sank into her reading chair, the leather creaking beneath her. The store felt different now - darker, heavier. Light from the streetlamp coming through the front window caused the cheerful window display she'd worked so hard on to cast long shadows across the floor. Her hands trembled when she lifted them to push back her curls.

Agatha's bell jingled as she trotted past, her tail held high. Christie followed close behind, both cats investigating the now-empty store as if nothing had changed.

The door to the non-fiction room gaped open like a wound. Rose pushed herself up from the chair, her legs unsteady. She had to close that door. Had to shut away what happened in there and get upstairs, into her own space. But as she approached the door, her vision swam. Was it her imagination, or could she smell the metallic scent of blood? At the thought, her knees buckled.

She dropped into a wooden chair in the hallway, pressing her palms against her eyes. She felt the band aid from her morning paper cut and shook her head. It seemed so silly now that she'd been upset by a paper cut. "I can't do this."

Agatha slipped past her into the darkened room. The cat's pale form glowed in the dim light as she prowled along the baseboards, whiskers twitching. She paused by one of the tall oak bookshelves, her paw darting behind it.

"Agatha, don't-" Rose's voice caught as Agatha batted something across the floor. A purple rubber band skittered across the hardwood. Something about it nagged at Rose's tired mind, but she couldn't focus enough to place why it seemed familiar.

Christie padded over to where the snow globe had shattered, her cream-colored nose working overtime as she investigated the spot. Broken glass and sparkling snow glittered in the moonlight. Christie stepped away, sniffing intently at a dark stain on the carpet.

"Christie, come away from there." Rose's stomach churned at the thought of blood, but as she stepped into the room to shoo her cats out, she paused. Christie continued sniffing the spot, and Rose, bending closer, noticed this stain looked different - darker, more brown. Like someone had spilled their coffee.

Chapter 5

Sunlight streamed through the front window of her bedroom, catching dust motes dancing in the air. Rose hadn't slept well, tossing and turning as her mind replayed the events of yesterday. The cheerful morning light felt wrong after what had happened.

A sharp knock at the front door downstairs made her jump.

Cocooned in warmth with Christie curled against her chest and Agatha stretched across her feet, Rose really didn't want to get up and face the day. She had every right to stay in bed and ignore the world today, she told herself.

But another knock echoed through the house, and with a sign, Rose untangled herself from the covers, trying not to disturb the cats.

Her hands shook as she pulled on jeans and a sweater. The wooden floors creaked beneath her bare feet as she hurried down the stairs, dark curls falling loose around her face.

At the bottom of the stairs, she froze. The closed door to the non-fiction room was to her left. Her chest tightened. She edged along the opposite wall, keeping her eyes fixed straight ahead.

This house was supposed to be her fresh start, her dream come true. The red exterior with its white trim had called to her the moment she'd first seen it. She'd spent weeks getting everything ready- painting the children's section that perfect sunny yellow, arranging reading nooks by the fireplace, creating a home for both books and readers.

But now someone had died here. Someone from this small town she barely knew but had already grown to love - where people brought welcome gifts and remembered your name, where kids rode bikes down Main Street and elderly couples walked hand-in-hand around the lake.

And one of those people was a murderer.

The thought made her stomach twist. She wrapped her arms around herself, the wool of her sweater soft against her palms. Christie and Agatha followed her to the front door and brushed against her legs. Their presence steadied her. This was still her home, still her dream. She wouldn't let fear steal that from her.

Another knock, more insistent this time.

Rose squared her shoulders and walked to the front door.

Officer Lindberg stood outside, her blonde ponytail gleaming in the sun. Rose's hands shook as she opened the door.

"Morning, Ms. Bennett." Officer Lindberg stepped inside, her snowy boots squeaking on the floor. "Do you mind if we sit?"

"Of course, come back to the kitchen."

As they settled at the kitchen table, Rose turned on the coffee pot. Officer Lindberg pulled out a small notepad. "Sorry to come by so early. But I need a list of everyone you can remember who was here for the grand opening yesterday. I'll be asking them all to come in for questioning. And you too, of course."

Rose nodded, filling coffee cups. Her hands were shaking, and coffee spilled on the counter. She remembered Jack, the vet, and his spilled coffee. It felt like a lifetime ago. "What time should I be there?"

"This afternoon. Two o'clock or so would be great." Officer Lindberg's blue eyes moved toward the front of the house, to the store. "Have you cleaned up in there yet?"

"No, I-" Rose swallowed hard. "I haven't been able to..."

"We're done processing the scene. You can clean it now." Officer Lindberg said gently. "And we can send someone over to help. I'm really sorry about this. This isn't the kind of welcome we generally give newcomers in whispering Pines."

Rose smiled. "Well, that's a relief. I'd be worried if this was the norm."

The officer tucked away her notepad. "I'll send Steve to help you clean. He's good. Does a great job. And I'll see you at two."

After the officer left, Rose forced herself to walk to the non-fiction room. The morning sun illuminated the stains on the carpet. She bent forward, studying the darker brown coffee stain next to the... other marks. Her vision swam and she stepped back, grabbing the doorframe for support. Why did there have to be blood?

"Thank heavens Steve is coming," she muttered to Agatha, pressing a hand to her churning stomach. "I'll need the help."

Rose grabbed her coat and purse from behind the counter. She needed air, needed to get away from the store for a while. Guilt gnawed at her for leaving the mess, but she couldn't face it right now. Not when her legs felt like jelly just looking at it.

She drove across town to the lake. It was frozen, glistening with snow in the morning light.

She parked, pulled on her hat, and set out to walk the path that circled the lake. It was over a mile and the cold air and brisk walk would clear her head.

As she walked, the snow made her think of the snow globe. Who had sent it? And who had used it to kill Professor Mitchell?

Back home, Rose filled two ceramic bowls with cat food, the familiar lunch-time routine steadying her nerves. Christie wound between her legs while Agatha watched from her perch on the kitchen counter.

"You two are comforting," she murmured, scratching Christie's ears. "Thank you for toughing this out with me." She smiled as Agatha brushed her leg on her way to the food bowl.

The drive to the police station was slow, her tires crunching through frozen snow. Downtown Whispering Pines looked like a postcard, white flakes dusting the Victorian storefronts and children pulling sleds along the sidewalk.

Inside the police station's cramped waiting room, familiar faces from yesterday's opening packed the space. The scent of coffee and pastries from Northern Pines Bakery filled the air. Chelsea Evans paced by the window, her work coveralls marked with fresh grease stains. She nodded at Rose before resuming her path.

Sarah Winters and Isabella Chang sat side by side, each reading, coffee cups in hand, napkins secured with rubber bands. Isabella was absorbed in paperback novel while Sarah appeared to be reading a manuscript, but before Rose could ask about it, Bridget hurried over.

"How are you holding up?" Bridget squeezed Rose's arm.

"I'm-" Rose started, but the office door opened.

Jack Hilton emerged and said good-bye to Officer Lindberg as he ran a hand through his already-mussed brown hair. "Thanks for your understanding, Jessie. Surgery at the clinic this afternoon." He paused when he saw Rose. "Oh, hey. How are the cats? And how are you holding up?"

"The cats are fine, thanks." She felt her cheeks warm as he smiled at her.

He nodded. "And you?"

She shook her head. "I don't know. It's a lot for opening day."

He gave her a small smile. "I'm sorry I've gotta go," he said. "Surgery. But I look forward to coming by later." He gave her arm a gentle squeeze before heading out the door.

As the door closed behind him, Rose remembered his visit yesterday, how he'd mentioned being notorious for spilling coffee. Her stomach dropped as she pictured the dark stain beside the broken snow globe. Spilled coffee. But Jack was so gentle with animals, so kind. She remembered him petting Agatha.

The image of Professor Mitchell's body flashed through her mind. She couldn't start suspecting people like Jack. Could she?

"Ms. Chang?" Officer Lindberg stood in her office doorway. Isabella looked up before she tucked her novel into her purse and followed Jessie inside, leaving her chair vacant.

Rose dropped into the chair and glanced at Sarah. Her gaze fell on Sarah's coffee cup, secured with a purple rubber band identical to the one Agatha had found behind the bookshelf. Her heart skipped.

"That rubber band," Rose said, her voice barely above a whisper. "Where did you get it?"

Sarah looked up from the papers she was reading, red pencil in one hand, eyebrows raised. "This?" She touched the band around her cup. "Northern Pines keeps them at the counter. Emma started doing it after too many people lost napkins in the snow." A small smile crossed her face. "Smart idea, really."

Rose's shoulders relaxed. Of course - that explained why the rubber band had seemed familiar.

"Did you know Professor Mitchell well?" The question slipped out before Rose could stop herself.

Sarah's smile faded. She looked down at her papers, her fingers tightening around the pages. "From school. Not very well though." Her voice caught slightly.

"I'm so sorry for your loss," Rose said, recognizing the pain in Sarah's expression. She knew what it felt like to lose someone, even if you weren't particularly close.

The office door opened again. "Ms. Bennett?" Officer Lindberg's voice carried across the waiting room.

Sarah looked up as Rose stood. "Good luck in there."

Rose's heart pounded as she walked toward Jessie's office.

Rose settled into the chair across from Officer Lindberg's desk, tucking her curls behind her ear. The office felt smaller than she'd expected, with case files stacked on metal cabinets and a coffee mug that read "World's Okayest Cop" on the corner of the desk.

"How are you holding up?" Jessie's blue eyes fixed on Rose's face. "Did you manage to get any sleep?"

"Some." Rose twisted her hands in her lap. "Christie and Agatha kept me company."

"Your cats?" At Rose's nod, Jessie leaned forward. "Tell me about your interactions with Professor Mitchell yesterday."

"He came in around ten. He was a little-" she winced at the thought of saying anything bad about someone who had been murdered. But this was an investigation. "He was a little abrupt. Even a bit rude, actually."

Jessie gave Rose a small smile. "That's Ed. You aren't the only one who's commented on that."

Rose nodded. "That's what Bridget said. He went into the non-fiction room looking at history books."

"Did you notice anyone else going into that room?"

Rose closed her eyes, picturing the day. "Chelsea bought a couple of Norse mythology books. Jack grabbed a book by James Herriot. Sarah went in briefly - I think she was looking for something specific."

"When did you notice the door was locked?"

Rose shook her head. "I didn't really, not while the shop was open. I didn't notice it until Christie started meowing at it after closing. I hadn't even realized it was closed, let alone locked." Rose's stomach clenched at the memory of what she'd found when she opened the door.

"Let's talk about the snow globe." Jessie made a note on her notepad. "It's an unusual murder weapon. Was it yours?"

"It was. It was a gift, for my grand opening, I think."

"What do you mean, you think."

"Well," Rose twisted her hands in her lap. "I don't actually know who sent it. I found it in a box on my doorstep that morning. There was a card, but it wasn't signed. I don't know who sent it."

Jessie stared at her. "It arrived that morning? And what did you do with it?"

"I put it in the window display, out front. And then I didn't see it again until I found— I mean, until…"

Jessie waited.

"Until I found the professor's body," Rose finished in a whisper.

"Interesting." Jessie made another note. "Forensics has it now. We'll see what the fingerprint analysis tells us. Thank you for coming in, Rose. I'll keep you posted. Let me know if you think of anything else, won't you?"

Chapter 6

Rose fumbled with her keys at the back door of The Literary Cat. The winter evening had already turned dark, and the streetlights cast long shadows across Main Street. She'd grabbed takeout from the diner, but her appetite vanished at the thought of returning to the store.

A truck pulled up behind her, headlights illuminating the alley.

"Need some help?" Steve climbed out, carrying a professional carpet cleaner. "Jessie mentioned you might need this."

Rose's shoulders sagged with relief. "You must be Steve. Thank you. I've been avoiding going back in there."

"That's what neighbors are for." He followed her inside, setting down the cleaner. "I brought sanitizer too. We'll get this cleaned up in no time."

Rose flipped on the lights, and Agatha darted over to investigate Steve's boots while Christie watched from her perch on the counter.

"I brought dinner if you're hungry." Rose gestured to the takeout bag. Her appetite was completely gone.

"Already ate, but thanks. Let's tackle the cleaning." Steve wheeled the cleaner toward the non-fiction room. "You don't have to look if you don't want to."

Rose took a deep breath. "No, I should help. It's my store."

Steve filled the cleaner's tank with hot water and sanitizer as Rose moved the love seat out of the way. The machine roared to life, sending both cats bolting up the stairs, tails puffed.

"Sorry girls!" Rose called after them.

"They'll forgive you." Steve shouted over the sound of the machine. "Especially if you bribe them with treats later." He gave her a wink.

Rose stood in the doorway, watching as the dark stains slowly disappeared under Steve's careful cleaning. Her stomach churned less with each pass of the machine.

"There." Steve switched off the cleaner. "Good as new. Though you might want to let it dry overnight."

"I can't thank you enough." Rose said. "I don't know what I would have done without your help."

"That's what small towns are for." Steve packed up the cleaner. "You going to be okay here tonight? Jessie- I mean Officer Lindberg- said she can come by and stay here tonight if you'd like."

"I think I'll be fine. Christie and Agatha are here, although at the moment they're probably hiding under my bed."

Steve laughed. "Cats. They're the best."

After Steve left, Rose stood in the doorway of the non-fiction room, taking in the now-clean carpet. Her cats crept down the stairs and wound around her ankles.

"Come on, girls. Let's get this room back in order."

She dragged the love seat back into position, then knelt to straighten the books on the bottom shelf.

As she reached behind the heavy oak bookcase to retrieve a fallen novel, her fingers brushed against paper.

"What's this?" She tugged at the corner but couldn't quite reach. "Christie, is this where you found that rubber band?"

Christie jumped onto the shelf above and peered down at Rose, tail swishing.

Rose braced her shoulder against the bookcase and pushed. The solid wood scraped across the carpet, revealing two crumpled pages. Her fingers could barely reach to pull them out. She stood and smoothed them out.

The pages were covered in neat typing with purple ink corrections in the margins. At the top, she read: "Dissertation Draft - Sarah Winters - Chapter 3."

Her phone rang, making her jump. Jack's name lit up the screen and her stomach did a little flip. she took a breath to steady her voice before answering.

"Hi Rose, hope I'm not calling too late." His warm voice filled the line. "Just wanted to check how you're holding up."

"Thank you. That's kind. I'm okay. Steve, from the police station, came by and helped me clean the carpet."

"Good. Listen, I'm finishing up at the clinic. Would it be alright if I stopped by for a minute? I've been worried about you."

Rose's heart skipped. She set down Sarah's pages and glanced at the now-clean spot on the carpet. Jack had mentioned spilling coffee often. Could he have...?

"Rose? You still there?"

"Yes, sorry. Of course you can stop by." She was being ridiculous imagining Jack could be the killer, she told herself as she tucked a curl behind her ear. "The cats would love to see you."

After hanging up, Rose hurried to the bathroom to check her reflection. She smoothed her sweater, ran fingers through her curls, and put on fresh lip gloss before catching herself.

"What am I doing? This isn't a date." She met Agatha's steady gaze in the mirror. "And he could be dangerous."

But Agatha just blinked at her, and Christie brushed Rose's leg with a purr.

Chapter 7

Rose checked the coffee pot for the third time before the doorbell chimed.

"Coming!" She took a breath and steadied herself. "This is ridiculous. He's neither a murderer nor a date. He's just a friendly vet."

She opened the door to find Jack on her snowy doorstep, his dark hair dusted with snowflakes. Her heart did that annoying little skip again.

"Come in before you freeze." She stepped back, watching his movements carefully. But he just stomped the snow from his boots and crouched to greet Christie, who had appeared to investigate.

"Hello beautiful girl." He scratched under Christie's chin as she purred. "And there's your sister."

Agatha emerged from behind the checkout counter, tail high.

"Would you like some coffee? I just made a fresh pot." Rose gestured toward the kitchen. "And I have cinnamon rolls from Northern Pines."

"That sounds perfect." Jack followed her, pausing to pet Agatha on his way to the kitchen. "I have some good news."

Rose poured coffee into two mugs.

"I thought it might be good to have something that might cheer you up after everything that's happened."

She handed him a mug, careful not to let their fingers brush. "Well, I could definitely use some cheering up."

"I've decided I can take Agatha and Christie as patients at my clinic."

"Really?" Rose's face lit up before she caught herself. "But I thought your practice was full?"

He reached down to stroke Christie, who had claimed her favorite cushion on the antique kitchen chair beside him. "After what happened yesterday... well, I wanted to do something to help."

"So, have you hired another vet tech, then?" Rose wrapped her hands around her coffee mug.

Jack shook his head with a wry smile and ran a hand through his hair, leaving it slightly messier than before. "I wish. I've been trying to hire someone since September. The closest qualified applicants are from Maple Grove or St. Cloud."

"That's quite a commute."

"Exactly. The last candidate took one look at the winter drive and declined." He broke off a piece of cinnamon roll. "I had someone lined up from Silver Pines, but she took a job closer to home last week."

"Isn't that a lot of work for you to do alone?"

Jack smiled. "It is, technically. But I've been thinking about you - about your situation, I mean. What happened yesterday. And today at the station..." He looked a bit flustered and took a sip of coffee. After he swallowed, he said, "I realized, I own the clinic. If I want to help a friend's pets, I can make that choice."

"Friends?" Rose set her mug down and looked at him. "We only just met yesterday, though it feels like forever ago."

Jack's warm brown eyes met hers. "I'd like to be friends, if that's okay with you?"

Rose stared into her coffee cup, her mind racing between Jack, and the word *friends*, and the spilled coffee by Professor Mitchell's body, and Jack cleaning the coffee in the main room of the shop. his words came back to her. *I'm so clumsy with coffee.*

"Can I ask you something?" Her fingers traced the rim of her mug.

"Of course." Jack leaned back in his chair, his expression open and warm.

"Earlier, you mentioned being clumsy with coffee cups. Did you mean that?"

His brow furrowed. "Unfortunately, yes. I've ruined more than one set of patient files that way." He gave a self-deprecating laugh. "Do you have a rule against being friends with clumsy people?"

Rose's heart sank. Was he a really good liar. He seemed so kind. But then, hadn't she read that murders often charm people?

To avoid his gaze, she glanced around the room. Her gaze fell on the trash bag propped by the kitchen door, still full of coffee cups from yesterday's grand opening.

"Hold on." She stood abruptly, making Christie jump from her perch. "I need to see..."

Rose crossed to the trash bag and undid the tie and opened it. Coffee cups. Dozens of them from the grand opening. Any one of them could have spilled beside Professor Mitchell. But she was looking for one thing in particular.

As she shifted through the cups and napkins, looking for any secured with a colorful rubber bands - like the purple one Agatha had found behind the bookshelf.

"Rose?" Jack's voice held concern. "What are you doing?"

She turned to face him and felt her cheeks turn red. "Quick question - Northern Pines Bakery keeps rubber bands at the counter for customers, right? For their napkins?"

"Yes, they do." Jack stood, looking puzzled. "Emma started doing that last winter when people kept dropping their napkins in the snow."

"What color are they? The rubber bands?"

"I don't understand-"

"Please, Jack. Just tell me - do they come in different colors?"

He shook his head slowly. "No, I don't think so. Just the regular brown ones, as far as I know. I've never seen colored ones there."

Rose nodded and sank back into her chair, her mind whirling with this information. "How sure are you?"

Jack shook his head, speechless, and just blinked at her.

Rose pulled out her phone, her fingers trembling slightly as she dialed Northern Pines Bakery.

"Northern Pines, this is Emma."

"Hi Emma, it's Rose from The Literary Cat."

"Rose! How are you holding up?"

"I'm okay. Quick question - the rubber bands you keep at the counter for napkins, what color are they?"

"Just plain brown ones. Why?"

Rose's heart pounded. "You've never had purple ones?"

"No, just brown. Always brown. Is everything alright?"

"Thanks Emma. I'll explain later."

Rose ended the call and immediately dialed the university History department. Jack watched her, his forehead creased with confusion.

"History department," a woman answered.

"Hi, I'm calling about Sarah Winters. She's a PhD candidate there?"

"Oh yes, Sarah. Wonderful news about her position at Stanford next fall. Professor Mitchell wrote such a glowing recommendation-"

Rose's breath caught. "Professor Mitchell? Did she know him then?"

There was a pause before the woman on the other end said, "Well of course. He was her advisor. They've worked together closely for the past three years. Everyone's devastated about what happened. My heart goes out to Sarah. Can I ask who's calling?"

Rose's phone slipped from fingers onto the table.

Jack picked it up and said into the phone, "We'll call you back." As Rose swayed slightly in her chair, he said, "Rose? Are you ok?"

She pushed back from the table, her chair scraping against the floor. Without answering, she hurried to the non-fiction room, carefully avoiding the damp spots on the carpet where Steve had cleaned the blood. Behind her, Jack's footsteps followed.

Rose retrieved the pages from where she'd left them lying on the shelf. For the first time, she really looked at the cramped handwriting filling the margins. Words jumped out at her: "uncited source," "direct copy," and there, underlined twice, a word that made her stomach feel like ice - "plagiarism."

She sank onto the loveseat, the pages trembling in her hands. Jack stood beside her, waiting.

"She said she didn't know him," Rose whispered. "Sarah lied."

Chapter 8

Rose shifted uncomfortably in her chair behind the two-way mirror, hyper-aware of Jack's presence beside her. The harsh fluorescent lights of the observation room cast strange shadows across Sarah's face through the glass as she faced Officer Lindberg.

Sarah crossed her legs, smoothing her pressed slacks. A purple rubber band circled her wrist. "I already told you yesterday, I barely knew Professor Mitchell."

"Then why did the department secretary say he was your advisor?" Officer Lindberg's voice crackled through the speaker.

"She must be mistaken." Sarah's fingers played with the rubber band. "I took one of his classes years ago, that's all."

Rose's stomach clenched. How did the lies flow so easily from Sarah's lips?

Jack placed his hand over hers, and only then did Rose realize how tightly she'd been gripping the chair.

Officer Lindberg motioned Rose into the interrogation room. Rose's legs felt shaky as she stepped through the door, clutching the evidence in her sweating palms.

Sarah's eyes widened. "What is she doing here?"

"Ms. Bennett has some information to share." Officer Lindberg pulled out a chair for Rose.

Rose placed the purple rubber band on the metal table. "I found this in the non-fiction room where Professor Mitchell died."

Sarah's brow furrowed. "A rubber band? That's your evidence?" She laughed, but it sounded hollow. "Northern Pines gives those to everyone for their coffee cups."

"Actually, they don't." Rose's voice grew stronger. "I called them. They only use plain brown ones."

Sarah's fingers went to the matching band on her wrist. "Fine. I use purple ones to keep track of my drinks. That doesn't mean anything."

Rose pulled out the wrinkled dissertation pages, smoothing them on the table. "Professor Mitchell made some interesting notes here about plagiarism."

The color drained from Sarah's face as her eyes locked onto the familiar handwriting.

"Our handwriting expert confirms these annotations match Professor Mitchell's writing samples," Officer Lindberg added.

Sarah's hands trembled. "This is ridiculous. I want to leave."

"There's more." Officer Lindberg opened a file. "The forensics report came back on the snow globe. Only three sets of prints were found - Ms. Bennett's, Izzy who left town the morning of the grand opening and caught a flight to Boston, and yours, Ms. Winters."

Sarah's carefully constructed facade cracked. She slammed her palm on the table, making Rose jump. "You don't understand what he was going to do to me! Everything I worked for - gone!"

Rose couldn't bear to watch Sarah's raw fury any longer. "Can I go?" she whispered to Officer Lindberg who nodded.

"Thank you, Rose."

Rose pushed back her chair and hurried out of the room, letting the door slam shut behind her, drowning Sarah's angry screams.

Rose stepped into the hallway, her heart pounding. Jack stood from his chair and wrapped her in a tight hug.

"That was incredible," he said. "The way you pieced it all together..."

Rose pulled back, her cheeks flushing. "I can't take all the credit. If Agatha hadn't found that rubber band, and Christie hadn't kept drawing my attention to the coffee stain..." She shook her head. "My cats helped solve my first mystery." she gave a shaky laugh.

Jack's eyes crinkled at the corners. "Your first? Planning on making this a habit?"

"Oh heavens, I hope not." Rose pressed a hand to her chest, feeling her heartbeat slow. "I really can't handle the sight of blood."

Officer Lindberg emerged from the interrogation room, leading Sarah out in handcuffs.

Sarah's perfect blonde hair had come loose from its clip, and her face was streaked with tears. She refused to look at Rose as they passed.

"Ready to head home?" Jack touched Rose's elbow.

Home. The word settled warm in Rose's chest. They walked out into the crisp night air, snowflakes dancing under the streetlights. Main Street looked like a scene from a Christmas card, or, she realized with a smile, a snow globe – wreaths in windows, twinkling lights strung between lamp posts, and a dusting of white coating the sidewalks.

The Literary Cat's front window glowed softly in the distance. Rose could make out Agatha and Christie in the display, undoubtedly wondering where she was. The sight of her bookstore, her cats waiting, and the steady presence of Jack, her new friend, beside her filled her with certainty.

"You know what?" Rose smiled up at Jack. "Despite everything that's happened, I think I've finally found where I belong."

"Whispering Pines has a way of doing that to people." Jack said, bumping her shoulder with his as they walked through the gently falling snow. "Welcome home, Rose."

Epilogue

A month after Sarah's arrest, Rose stood behind the counter of The Literary Cat, warmth spreading through her chest as she watched familiar faces fill her shop for the grand re-opening. Sunlight streamed through the freshly cleaned windows, catching the sparkle of fresh snow outside on Main Street.

"Rose, I have something for you." Izzy approached the counter, a wrapped package in her hands. Her cheeks were pink from the cold.

"Oh my gosh. Izzy, you didn't!" Rose unwrapped the gift carefully, revealing a stunning snow globe featuring Whispering Pines' historic Main Street. There, in miniature, stood The Literary Cat, its red walls and white trim perfect down to the tiny books visible in the window display.

"Izzy, it's beautiful." Rose turned it over in her hands. "But you didn't need to get one again. This must have cost-"

"Don't even think about it." Izzy waved away her concern. "I feel terrible about rushing off to that conference without signing the card on the first one. I had no idea it would become..." She trailed off.

"Evidence?" Rose finished with a small smile.

Agatha stretched lazily on her new velvet cushion beside the register, accepting a treat from Isabella while Christie batted playfully at the ends of Izzy's scarf.

"These two deserve medals," Officer Lindberg said, scratching Christie behind the ears. "Maybe we should deputize them as official police consultants."

"Special cakes for special cats!" Bridget called as she swept in carrying a tray of cupcakes, each topped with detailed fondant books and tiny cats.

The bell above the door jingled again and Jack stepped in, shaking snow from his coat.

Rose stepped away from the counter to greet him. She held out a hand, but her pulled her in for a quick hug.

"Just wanted to wish you luck before heading to the clinic." His eyes crinkled as he smiled at Rose.

From the corner of her eye, Rose saw Izzy raise an eyebrow at Jack's greeting.

"Thank you. I hope work is great today! Will you stop by after work? We're having a game night, and I'd love to have you join us."

"Wouldn't miss it."

Rose watched him leave, then set the new snow globe carefully in the front window before turning and taking in the scene before her - books lined neatly on warm wooden shelves, soft classical music playing, the scent of coffee and fresh pastries mingling in the air. Her neighbors chatted and browsed, their laughter filling the space with joy. This was everything she'd dreamed of when she'd first imagined opening a bookstore.

Christie jumped onto the counter, purring as she rubbed against Rose's hand before attempting to lick frosting from a cupcake.

"Oh, no you don't," Rose said.

Agatha followed, settling regally beside her sister. Rose scratched them both behind their ears, knowing without a doubt that coming to Whispering Pines had been the right decision - even with the murder mystery she never expected to solve.

Read all Penelope Loveletter's Books!

www.Penelope Loveletter.com

lots of love,

Penelope

LOVELETTER
PUBLICATIONS

EST. 2023

Printed in Great Britain
by Amazon